TRICK OR TREAT, IT'S HALLOWEEN!

By Linda Lowery
and Richard Keep

A Random House PICTUREBACK® Book

Random House 🏠 New York

Copyright © 2000 by Fudrick and Friends, Inc.
All rights reserved under International and Pan-American Copyright
Conventions. Published in the United States by Random House, Inc., New York,
and simultaneously in Canada by Random House of Canada Limited, Toronto.
ISBN: 0-375-80617-2

www.randomhouse.com/kids

Library of Congress Catalog Card Number: 00-132681
Printed in the United States of America   August 2000   10 9 8 7 6 5 4 3
PICTUREBACK, RANDOM HOUSE and colophon, and PLEASE READ TO ME and colophon
are registered trademarks of Random House, Inc.

NOV 28 2000

Apples dunked in caramel goo

Bats out playing peekaboo

Cats come creeping, black and lean
Oh my gosh! It's Halloween!

Darkness brings its bone-white stars

Earthlings dress like men from Mars

Faces turn to ghouly green
Grab a mask! It's Halloween!

Ghosts and goblins arm in arm

Home becomes a pumpkin farm

Imps and critters watch and wait

Jack-o'-lanterns guard the gate

Kids paint bags for candy treats

Lanterns light up spooky streets

Mummies rise from the ravine
Out you go! It's Halloween!

Night winds wail through neighborhoods.

Owls keep watch from haunted woods

Pirates swagger, panthers prowl

Queens parade and werewolves howl

Ravens dive for pumpkin seeds

Skeletons skulk through the weeds

Tales are told of spooks unseen
Boo! Beware! It's Halloween!

Urchins begging by the bunch

Witches offer broomstick rides

marks where a treasure hides

Yikes! A yawning sleepyhead!

Zombies zigzag home to bed

Will your creepy face come clean?

Linda Lowery AND Richard Keep

are married and live on a pumpkin farm in Boulder, Colorado, with their son, Kris, and their furry-faced cat, Max. Linda has written children's books for twenty years, and Rick has taught high school art for just as long. Rick had a great time cutting and pasting the menagerie of monsters in this book, since Halloween is his favorite holiday. Linda's favorite part of Halloween is the extra candy left in the treat bowl at the end of the night.